Lena Landström

The New Hippos

Translated by Joan Sandin

R&S
BOOKS

Stockholm   New York   London   Adelaide   Toronto

Something's happened down by the riverbank where the hippos live.

The big hippos, who are usually relaxing in the warm water, don't know which way to turn. And the lively little hippos, who love to dive, have completely forgotten about their diving board. And Mrs. Hippopotamus, who always makes seaweed pudding for dinner, has burned her pudding. Things are not at all as they usually are. Something is disturbing the hippos . . .

Two new hippos have arrived!

Nice riverbank, they think. Lots of room. And a diving board!

"Can I dive, too?" asks the new little hippo.
"No," answer the other little hippos.
"No way."
"You're too little."
"It's too dangerous."

All day the new little hippo watches the other
little hippos diving and having fun.
The new hippo mama has started building a hut.

The next morning, when the little hippos are on their way
to the diving board, they get a big surprise.

They rush down to the water, and the new little hippo
comes swimming toward them.
"How did you do that?"
"Show us!"
"Is it hard to do?"

It is hard. The new little hippo shows them over and over, and the little hippos try it again and again. After lots of practice, they are able to spin around in the air and dive into the water. But the new little hippo spins the fastest.

Meanwhile, the new hippo mama is hard at work building her hut. She spreads out the sticks and gets tangled up in the vines. The big hippos watch.
"We've never done it like that," they say to each other.
"It probably won't last very long."

Mrs. Hippopotamus, who lives alone and is used to building things, offers her toolbox.

A few days later the new hut is finished.

The big hippos think it looks pretty sturdy.

One morning, when the little hippos meet at the diving board,
the new little hippo isn't there.

He isn't in his hut either. No one is there.
"Have they moved? Didn't they like the riverbank?" the big
hippos wonder.
"No, their suitcase is still here," say the little hippos.
Something terrible must have happened!
"Maybe you should look for them!" shouts Mrs. Hippopotamus
from her hut.

The little hippos go off into the jungle to look.
They search the Dark Cave.

They search down by the crocodiles.

And they search the Poison Pool. There's
not a trace of the new hippos to be found.

"They're gone!" they say to the big hippos. "We can't find them anywhere!"
Just then they hear some groaning and panting in the trees.

They're back!

The new little hippo and his mama are carrying a bundle full of delicious jungle fruit. It's enough for everybody.

The new hippos promise they will always tell someone before they leave the riverbank.

Once again, everything is the way it's always been down by the riverbank.

The little hippos have become really good at doing somersaults from the diving board—almost as good as the new little hippo.

The hippo mama is reading in her lounge chair.

Suddenly she has trouble concentrating on her book.
Something feels wrong. Who is that talking?
"Nice riverbank!"
"Lots of room!"
"And a diving board!"

Three new hippos have arrived!